Mel Bay's Christmas Carols For Recorder

by Franz Zeidler

FOREWORD

Music provides one of the most satisfying ways of celebrating the joyous Christmas season.

The warmth and joy are so much part of this season that words alone cannot express the sincere and profound feelings, people therefore put their thoughts to music.

The selections in this booklet are Christmas songs and carols, from many different countries, which have proven to be so proper for the season that, to perform these lovely short compositions, has become a very enjoyable tradition.

Season's Greetings! **Franz Zeidler**

TABLE OF CONTENTS

O COME, O COME EMMANUEL

PLAINSONG MELODY
11th Century

BESIDE THE CRADLE HERE I STAND

J. S. BACH

In Choral Style

HE SHALL FEED HIS FLOCK

ARIA from the Oratorio THE MESSIAH

G. F. HANDEL

HE IS BORN

FRENCH NOEL

TRADITIONAL

FROM HEAVEN ABOVE

from GEISTLICHE LIEDER, Leipzig, 1539

MARTIN LUTHER
1535

WE HAIL THEE WITH REJOICING

W. A. MOZART

HOW VAIN THE CRUEL HEROD'S FEAR

HEINRICH SCHÜTZ

NOËL

from A COLLECTION OF 18th CENTURY FRENCH
CHRISTMAS SONGS by ESPRIT PHILIPPE CHEDEVILLE

GRACE SOIT RENDUE

from CHEDEVILLE'S COLLECTION

BON JOSEPH, ECOUTE – MOI

from CHEDEVILLE'S COLLECTION

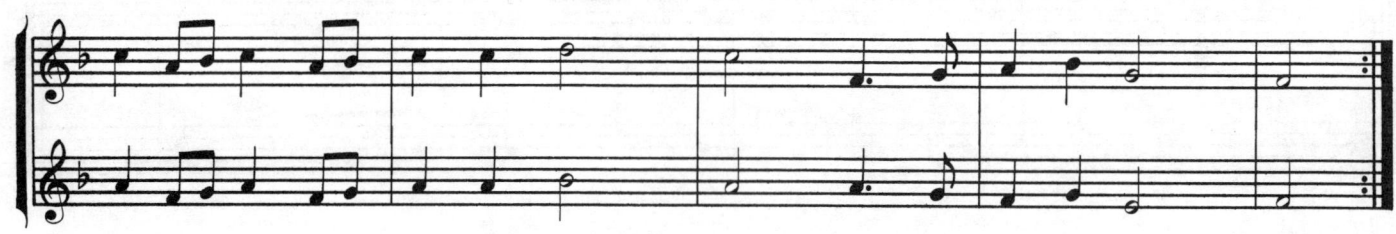

POUR L'AMOUR DE MARIE

from CHEDEVILLE'S COLLECTION

JOSEPH, O DEAR JOSEPH MINE

GERMAN TRADITIONAL

11th Century

9

RING CHRISTMAS BELLS

UKRANIAN CAROL

LEONTOVICH

KOMMET IHR HIRTEN
GERMAN TRADITIONAL CHRISTMAS CAROL

Postlude *(ad libitum)*

HARK! THE HERALD ANGELS SING

FELIX MENDELSSOHN

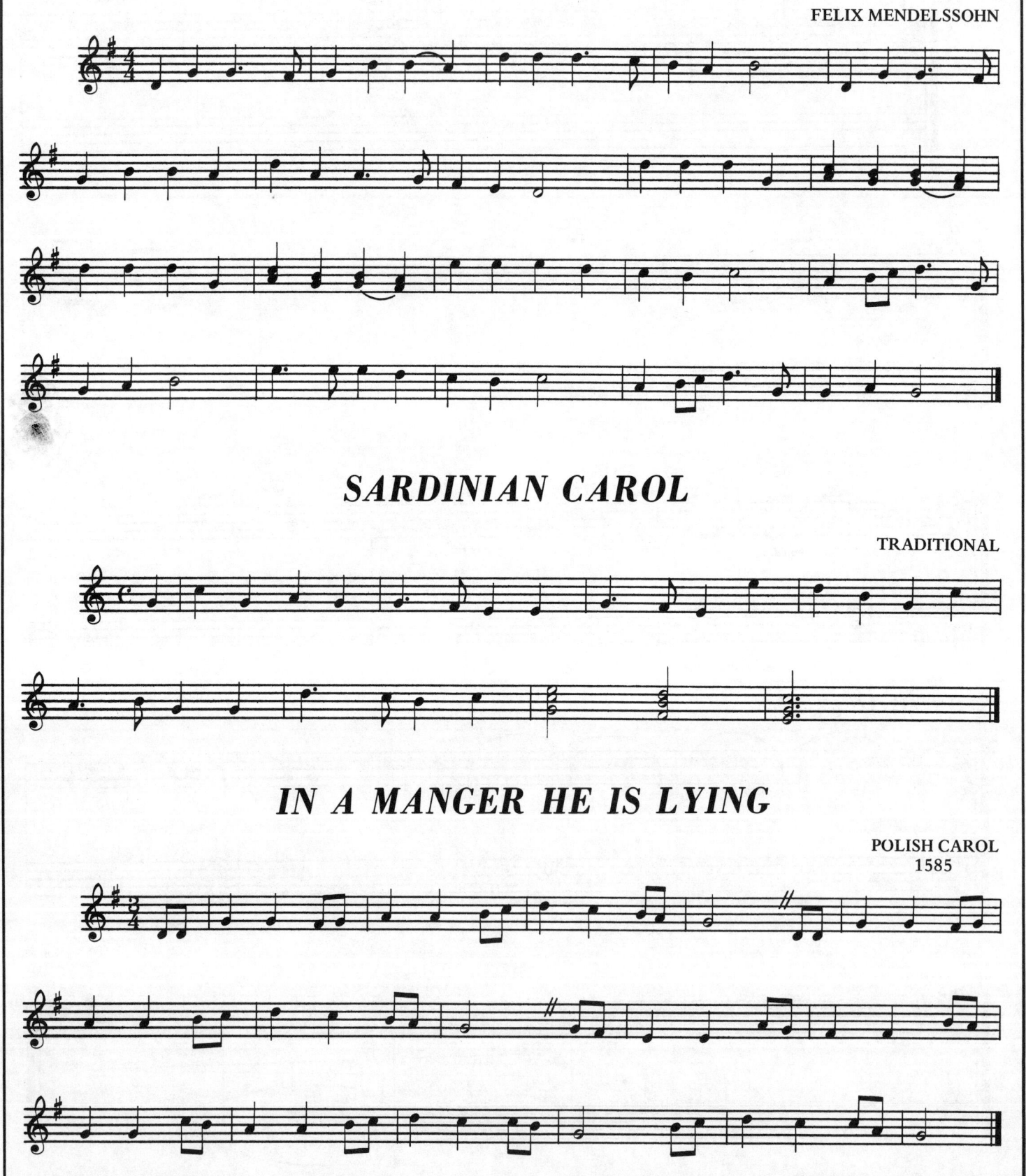

SARDINIAN CAROL

TRADITIONAL

IN A MANGER HE IS LYING

POLISH CAROL
1585

SILENT NIGHT

GERMAN CAROL

FRANZ GRUBER

(small notes ad lib.)

GOOD CHRISTIAN MEN REJOICE

ANONYMOUS
13th Century

AS LATELY WE WATCHED

BAVARIAN TRADITIONAL

ANONYMOUS

COMPANIONS, ALL SING LOUDLY

TRADITIONAL BASQUE CAROL

ANONYMOUS

IN A SILENT WINTER NIGHT

GERMAN TRADITIONAL

ADORAMUS TE CHRISTE

GIOVANNI DA PALESTRINA